Other books by Mick Inkpen:

One Bear at Bedtime
The Blue Balloon
Threadbear
Lullabyhullaballoo!
Penguin Small
Nothing
Bear
The Great Pet Sale

The Wibbly Pig books
The Kipper books
The Blue Nose Island books

First published in 1991
by Hodder Children's Books.
This edition published in 2007

Copyright © Mick Inkpen 1991

Hodder Children's Books
338 Euston Road, London NW1 3BH

Hodder Children's Books Australia
Level 17/207 Kent Street, Sydney, NSW 2000

A catalogue record of this book is
available from the British Library.

ISBN: 978 0 340 93110 3
10 9 8 7 6 5 4 3

Printed in China

Hodder Children's Books is a
division of Hachette Children's Books.
An Hachette Livre UK Company.

www.hachettelivre.co.uk

Billy's
Beetle

Mick Inkpen

Hodder
Children's
Books

A division of Hachette Children's Books

Billy had a beetle in a matchbox.
Or rather he hadn't. He had lost it.
Silly Billy.

'Have you seen my beetle?' he asked
the girl. But she hadn't.

Along came a man with a sniffy dog.

'Don't you worry!' said the man with the sniffy dog. 'My sniffy dog will soon find your beetle!'

Off went the sniffy dog.

Sniff. Sniff. Sniff.

Soon the sniffy dog had found a hedgehog,
two spiders, some worms and a bone.
But not the beetle.

'I will help find Billy's beetle,' said the
hedgehog. And so the search continued.

Suddenly, the sniffy dog stopped digging
and took off like a rocket!

'Look at him go!' said the man.
'He can smell Billy's beetle!'

But the sniffy dog had not smelled Billy's beetle.
He had smelled sausages.

    'Leave, sniffy dog! Leave!' said the man.
So the sniffy dog grabbed the sausages,
and left!

Now there was Billy, the girl, the hedgehog,
the sniffy dog, the man with the sniffy dog,
and the woman without the sausages,
all looking for Billy's beetle.
(And a polar bear who had joined in for fun.)

The sniffy dog found a tuba. It belonged to a man in the oompah band.

'I don't think Billy's beetle is in there,' said the bandsman. 'But we will help you look.'

So the oompah band played and off they went again. Oompah! Oompah! Sniff, sniff, sniff!

An elephant wandered over to see what all
the fuss was about.

'Stand aside!' said the man with the sniffy dog.
'My sniffy dog is looking for this boy's beetle!'
The elephant became very excited.

'I've seen it!' he said.

The elephant jumped up and down and pointed
with his trunk.

‘Is THAT the beetle?’ he trumpeted triumphantly.

‘No,’ said Billy. ‘That is not my beetle.
That is a furry caterpillar.’

Instantly the elephant was untriumphant and untrumpetible. He sat down.

The girl sighed a long, long sigh and sat down too.

'Where can it be?' she said.

The man with the sniffy dog, the sniffy dog, the lady without the sausages, the polar bear and the oompah band sat down next to them.

But the hedgehog was hopping from one foot to the other, and pointing.

'The beetle! It's the beetle!'
he squeaked.

'We've found the beetle! We've found the beetle!'
'HOORAY! HOORAY! HOORAY!' they shouted.

'BUT WHERE IS BILLY?' said the girl.
Everybody stopped shouting. They looked up.
They looked down. They looked behind, in front,
and in between. But Billy had disappeared.

'Don't you worry!' said the man with the
sniffy dog. 'My sniffy dog has found something!'

But the sniffy dog had not found Billy.
He had found a little pig.

'Excuse me,' said the little pig.
'I have lost my furry caterpillar.
Have you seen him?'

So the girl, the sniffy dog, the man with the
sniffy dog, the hedgehog, the woman without the
sausages, the polar bear, the oompah band,
the elephant, the little pig AND the beetle
all went off together to look for Billy
and the furry caterpillar.

And once again
it was the hedgehog
who found them...

...and the sniffy dog who didn't!